WARNING!

Scaredy Squirrel insists that everyone put on mittens before reading this Safety Guide.

Mélanie Watt

Scaredy Squirrel

prepares for

CHRISTMAS

KIDS CAN PRESS

MÉLANIE WATT PRODUCTIONS

This **Safety Guide** is now in your hands. You must promise to protect it from:

- germs
- volcanoes
- bathtubs

Please note that this book is not for:

A. monsters

B. vampire bats

C. killer bees

D. lobsters

CONTENTS

BUT FIRST,
A WORD
FROM
SCAREDY
SQUIRREL:

Safety

....

SCAREDY SQUIRREL
IN A NUTSHELL

IDENTIFICATION FORM

Name: SCAREDY ORVILLE SQUIRREL

Initials: S.O.S.

Born: OCTOBER 3RD

at: 13:28 HOURS AND 6 SECONDS in NUT TREE.

Likes: PROTECTIVE GEAR, SCHEDULES, PLANS AND SAFETY GUIDES

Dislikes: GERMS, DANGER AND MAKING EYE CONTACT, TO NAME A FEW

Pet peeves: UNKNOWN STUFF IN GENERAL

Folder
(this squirrel's best friend)

Safety kit
(a classic)

Safety goggles
(a must)

Hard hat
(a no-brainer)

Safety pin

Rubber gloves
(a genius invention)

INTRODUCTION

Christmas is sneaking up around the corner!
If you don't want to be taken by surprise,
it's important you keep a close eye
on what's going on around you.
Always stay one step ahead of the game!

STEP 1: Panic

STEP 2: Take a deep breath

STEP 3: Pace around in circles

STEP 4: Locate a mirror

STEP 5: Check your teeth for gingerbread

STEP 6: Look closely at yourself

STEP 7: Take a personality quiz ...

THE SCAREDY

1. The Christmas holidays make me ...

happy ☐ (0 points)

jolly ☐ (0 points)

panic ☐ (1 point)

2. This year I was ...

naughty ☐ (0 points)

nice ☐ (0 points)

nervous ☐ (1 point)

3. Decorating makes me ...

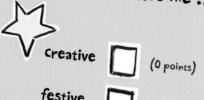

creative ☐ (0 points)

festive ☐ (0 points)

anxious ☐ (1 point)

4. Dashing through the snow ...

in a one horse open sleigh ☐ (0 points)

sounds dangerous ☐ (1 point)

CHRISTMAS QUIZ

5. My tree must be ...

real ☐ (0 points)

fake ☐ (0 points)

germ-free ☐ (1 point)

6. Fruitcake makes a ...

great gift ☐ (0 points)

tasty dessert ☐ (0 points)

good paper weight ☐ (1 point)

7. On the first day of Christmas, my true love gave to me ...

a partridge in a pear tree ☐ (0 points)

sorry, I don't socialize ☐ (1 point)

8. What do you see?

a cute reindeer ☐ (0 points)

a dangerous creature with antlers from outer space with a red-nose tracking device ☐ (1 point)

IMPORTANT!
If, like Scaredy, your total points range between 1 and 8, this Safety Guide is in fact for you!

CHRISTMAS

Aries (March 21–April 19)
You can climb snow-covered mountains and achieve anything during the holidays!

Taurus (April 20–May 20)
Time to beef up the decorations. Express your joy in every way!!

Gemini (May 21–June 21)
Double the Christmas spirit and double the holiday fun!

Cancer (June 22–July 22)
Red is your color. You'll stand out during the Christmas season!

Leo (July 23–Aug. 22)
Relax, last-minute Christmas shopping is nothing to growl about!

Virgo (Aug. 23–Sept. 22)
Everyone thinks you're an angel. Be proud of yourself and sing!

HOROSCOPES

Libra (Sept. 23–Oct. 23)

Weigh the pros and cons before you choose those Christmas gifts!

Scorpio (Oct. 24–Nov. 21)

Try not to be picky about your holiday cooking — everyone loves you!

Sagittarius (Nov. 22–Dec. 21)

You're pointing in the right direction. You'll have fun this holiday season!

Capricorn (Dec. 22–Jan. 19)

You have the best of both worlds. It's the most wonderful time of the year!

Aquarius (Jan. 20–Feb. 18)

Don't freeze — it's the perfect time of the year to go caroling!

Pisces (Feb. 19–March 20)

You glitter with your bubbly personality. You'll be the life of the Christmas party!

ABOUT THIS SAFETY GUIDE

Greetings, festive readers.
Christmas is indeed the most wonderful
time of the year, but it is also the scariest!

Which is why I, Scaredy Squirrel,
have developed this trusty Safety Guide.

Divided into eight easy chapters, this book
is designed to help you prepare for and survive
the Christmas holidays, one page at a time!

Now, let's begin!

S.o.S.

CHAPTER 1

CHRISTMAS IS
COMING

Before tackling the holidays, you will need to gear up with a few safety items:

A SCAREDY TIP!
Gathering these items in August is your best bet. It will avoid last-minute disasters.

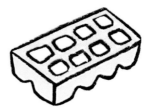

ice cube tray

traffic cones

chamomile tea

boots

antibacterial soap
(green for a festive look)

spotlight

soup

hair dryer

Saint Bernard

hockey helmet

yoga mat

shovel

THE HOLIDAY PLAN

Your safety gear will come in handy when you encounter the usual holiday obstacles!

OBSTACLE LEGEND

 ICE STORMS

 STRESS

 AVALANCHES

 SHOPPING TRAFFIC

 RUNAWAY TOBOGGANS

 COLD GERMS

 ABOMINABLE SNOWMAN

 ICE-CLEANING MACHINES

 TIME

Lure away the monstrous ice-cleaning machines with a trail of irresistible ice cubes!

Use a spotlight to spot the obstacles!

CHRISTMAS IS HERE!

Relax with yoga!

Drink tea to calm the nerves of last-minute shopping!

You can never have too much hot soup to wash away the cold season!

Use a shovel to build an igloo and take shelter from runaway toboggans!

If faced with a demanding Abominable Snowman, melt the troubles away with a hair dryer. That should blow him off!

CHRISTMAS IS HERE!

Have a reliable Saint Bernard on call **24-7** in case panic triggers an avalanche!

YOU ARE HERE

Direct shopping traffic away with a few well-placed cones!

Wear a hockey helmet. The goal is to avoid getting knocked out by ice storm pellets!

CHRISTMAS IS HERE!

Race against the clock! These boots are made for running and there's a lot to do!

12 THINGS TO DO

BEFORE CHRISTMAS
(The Countdown)

12	Lift weights (to be fit to carry heavy packages)
11	Practice standing in one spot (for long line-ups)
10	Iron tuxedo (to look spiffy)
9	Weigh piggy bank (to balance budget)
8	Do finger stretches (to prepare for holiday crafting)
7	Take voice lessons (to sing Christmas carols on key)

6	Run on treadmill (to keep up with the holiday rush)
5	Get annual eye exam (to keep focus)
4	Clean ears (to listen for sugarplum fairies)
3	Have a make-over (to win compliments)
2	Floss (to prevent cavities from eating holiday sweets)
1	Repeat all of the above (because repetition is good)

CHAPTER 2

CHRISTMAS DECORATIONS

CRAFTING SAFETY 101

Football helmet:
Headgear protects from
falling Christmas ornaments

Flashlight:
Adequate work
lighting is a must

Mittens:
To shield against
paper cuts

Painter's suit:
In case things
get messy

Radio:
Christmas music helps
set the mood

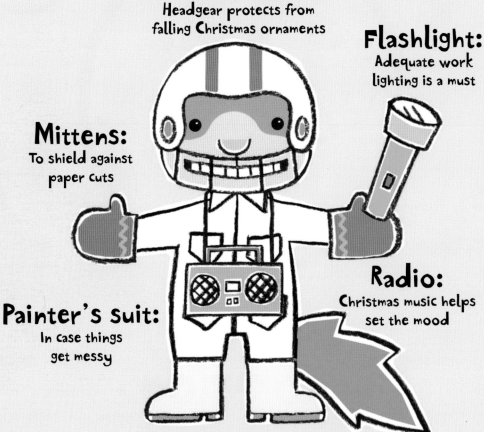

Rubber rain boots:
Footgear in case you're flooded with creative ideas

FOR THE AdVanCed CRAFTER ...

DRAWING WITH MARKERS

Warning!
Not for doubters.
This demands a good, steady paw. There's no turning back!

permanent marker

CRAFTING A SNOWMAN GARLAND

Attention!
Not for beginners.
Experience needed. Plus, never run with, near or into scissors.

rounded scissors

KNITTING CHRISTMAS STOCKINGS

Important!
Holiday-colored yarn can attract bobcats.

safety goggles

DECORATING YOUR TREE FOR THE CHRISTMAS HOLIDAYS:

Not festive

TIDY UP!

1. Store away any debris that doesn't look festive.

TREE PLAN
CLIENT: S.O.S.

- CM
- INCHES

Christmas tree blueprint

2. Draw a plan.

3. Select the perfect shades
of red and green.

SCAREDY'S TREE

4. Find decorations that meet
Scaredy's safety regulations:

 A. Handle sharp-edged
ornaments with
caution

 B. Solar-powered
lights only

 C. Plastic, not glass

 D. Fake berries
so they will not
attract wild cardinals

5. Decorate with caution
(No ladders, please!!!)

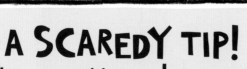

A SCAREDY TIP!
Not everything red or green
is safe to use as a
holiday decoration!

A few RED things to avoid decorating with:

dynamite

street signs

chili peppers

dragons

poisonous berries

fire hydrants

A few **GREEN** things to avoid decorating with:

Martians

tons of
air fresheners

catnip

caterpillars

poison ivy

bullfrogs

CHAPTER 3

HOLIDAY
SWEETS

THE PROS OF
HOLIDAY SWEETS:

THE FRUITCAKE

- Generous fruit and nut serving
- Colorful and festive
- Lasts for decades

THE CANDY CANE

- Portable
- Makes an attractive ornament
- Comes in hygienic plastic wrap

THE CHRISTMAS LOG

- Amazing work of art (It looks so real!)
- Feeds many
- Great conversation piece

THE CONS OF HOLIDAY SWEETS:

THE FRUITCAKE

- Requires a sturdy table
- Very popular re-gift item
- Lasts for decades

THE CANDY CANE

- Will lead to dental appointments
- Will stick to fur and toupees
- Could shatter into a million pieces

THE CHRISTMAS LOG

- Not appetizing (It looks too real!)
- Might invite termites
- Needs chainsaw for slicing

BUILDING A STURDY "TO CODE" GINGERBREAD HOUSE

Using the items below:

white glue

glue stick

duct tape

fan

varnish

carrot

1. Bake gingerbread walls and roof.

2. Get a building permit.

3. Assemble house using glue and tape.

4. Varnish and let dry.
(It's guaranteed — this beauty isn't going anywhere!)

A SCAREDY TIP!
Remember, this gingerbread house is pleasing to the eye but not the stomach!

PLEASE NOTE: Carrot is for snacking on while waiting for everything to dry.

SETTING A HYGIENIC DESSERT TABLE

1 Find a table and disinfect it from top to bottom.
(Germs thrive in cracks!)

2 Verify table sturdiness using a level tool.
(Wobbly legs can result in disaster!)

3 Select an elegant tablecloth.
(Plaid is best to represent the holiday theme!)

4 Position desserts carefully on the table.
(In clockwise, alphabetical order for efficiency!)

5 Display the plates and cutlery.
(Round edges only ... for safety!)

6 Provide guests with handy cleaning items.
(Festive napkins, hand wipes and toothbrushes!)

P.S. Position cones for optimal guest traffic flow!

CHAPTER 4

CHRISTMAS
GIFTS

SHOPPING FOR THE DIFFICULT INDIVIDUALS IN YOUR LIFE

A SCAREDY TIP!

When you identify the specific personality types of your loved ones, gift ideas come more easily.

THE SILENT TYPE

GIFT IDEAS:
- Tickets to a silent movie
- TV remote with mute button
- Earmuffs

THE UPTIGHT TYPE

GIFT IDEAS:
- Spa treatment certificate
- Sounds of the ocean **CD**
- Yoga lessons

THE MYSTICAL TYPE

GIFT IDEAS:
- Magic kit for beginners
- Glittery stuff
- Reliable horoscope book

THE SENSITIVE TYPE

GIFT IDEAS:
- Cashmere sweater
- Feel-good movie
- Monogrammed handkerchief

THE ELUSIVE TYPE

GIFT IDEAS:
*Don't even bother with this one; he's nowhere to be seen.

THE OUTDOORSY TYPE

GIFT IDEAS:
- Toothpicks
- Compass and GPS
- Survival kit

THE HAIRY TYPE

GIFT IDEAS:
- Waxing kit
- Nose-hair trimmer
- Vacuum

THE TRANSPARENT TYPE

GIFT IDEAS:
- Beret
- Elegant silk tie
- Freestanding mirror

THE STINGING TYPE

GIFT IDEAS:
- Balloons
- Flower arrangement
- One-way ticket to a faraway place

THE HARDHEADED TYPE

GIFT IDEAS:
- Gift card
- 3D puzzle
- Pillow

THE FUNNY TYPE

GIFT IDEAS:
- Whoopee cushion
- Rubber chicken
- Banana peel

THE WORKER TYPE

GIFT IDEAS:
- Vacation
- Filing cabinet
- Novelty coffee mug

THE GRUMPY TYPE

GIFT IDEAS:
- Ticket to an offbeat Broadway musical
- Salsa dance lessons
- Table for one at a nice restaurant

THE FRIENDLY TYPE

GIFT IDEAS:
- Friendship bracelet
- Homemade cookies
- Candy cane-scented air freshener

THE SCAREDY TYPE

GIFT IDEAS:
- Nothing scary
- Nothing unsafe
- Nothing flammable

GIFT WRAPPING

TO: S.O.S.
FROM: S.O.S.

Exhibit A:

1. Measure the gift box. (Square shape works best.)

2. Measure twice. (You can never be too careful!)

3. Cut wrapping paper 1.56 times bigger than the gift box. (Paper pattern should be thematic and festive.)

4. Fold paper over box. (Perfect horizontal creases work best.)

5. Tape down. (Use transparent tape so it blends in.)

6. Place decorative bow. (Make it match and don't get tied up.)

7. Attach name tag. (To avoid embarrassing mix-ups.)

OTHER GIFT PACKAGES MAY INCLUDE ...

stockings

PROS: Attractive
CONS: Smell like feet

paper bags

PROS: Cute and recyclable
CONS: Items can fall out

gift cards

PROS: Lightweight
CONS: Lack pizzazz

UNSUITABLE CANDIDATES FOR WRAPPING:

crustaceans

four-legged mammals

trees

A SCAREDY TIP!
To avoid sticky fingers,
put on oven mitts before you
proceed to wrap.

CHAPTER 5

CHRISTMAS CHARACTERS

SANTA CLAUS

(Who is this guy and what does he want?)

THE HAT:
Says he's bold and bald

THE BUTTON NOSE:
Smells cookies from miles away!

THE RED SUIT:
Quality velvet, hand stitched by Mrs. Claus herself

THE BELT:
Holds everything in, which is essential for fitting into chimneys

THE POM-POM:
Shows his playful side

THE BEARD:
Well trimmed and white as snow

gloves = no germs

THE JOLLY BELLY:
Direct result of eating too many cookies

THE BOOTS: Always polished, never covered in soot

HIS MISSION: To deliver presents to well-behaved kids all around the world!

SAFETY BACKGROUND CHECK

NAME: Mr. Santa Claus A.K.A. Saint Nicholas

MARITAL STATUS: Married

SPOUSE: Mrs. Claus (wears matching outfit)

RESIDENCE: North Pole

VEHICLE: Sled equipped with 8 reindeer and 1 headlight (Rudolph)

COMMON EXPRESSION: Ho! Ho! Ho! (multilingual)

FAVORITE TIME OF YEAR: Christmas Eve (December 24th)

FAVORITE HANGOUT: The mall

THUMBPRINTS:

EXHIBIT A:
SANTA'S LIST

	NAUGHTY	NICE
BUDDY	☐	☑
SCAREDY SQUIRREL	☐	☑
CHESTER (the cat)	☐	☑ ☒
SEA MONSTER	☑	☐
GERMS	☑	☐
MÉLANIE WATT	☐	☑
BIGFOOT	☑	☐

INTERESTING SANTA FACTS:

- Makes lists, checks them twice (Scaredy Squirrel approves)

- Is often mentioned in songs and books

- Reads a ton of letters (literally)

- Not claustrophobic (chimneys)

- Doesn't work alone; has helpers

THE ELF

(according to Scaredy Squirrel)

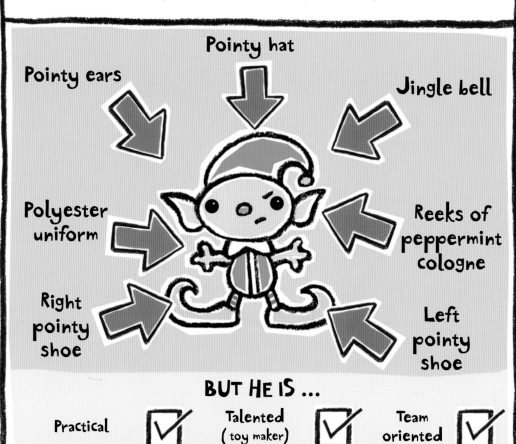

Pointy hat

Pointy ears

Jingle bell

Polyester uniform

Reeks of peppermint cologne

Right pointy shoe

Left pointy shoe

BUT HE IS ...

Practical ✓ Talented (toy maker) ✓ Team oriented ✓

THE REINDEER

(Rudolph according to Scaredy Squirrel)

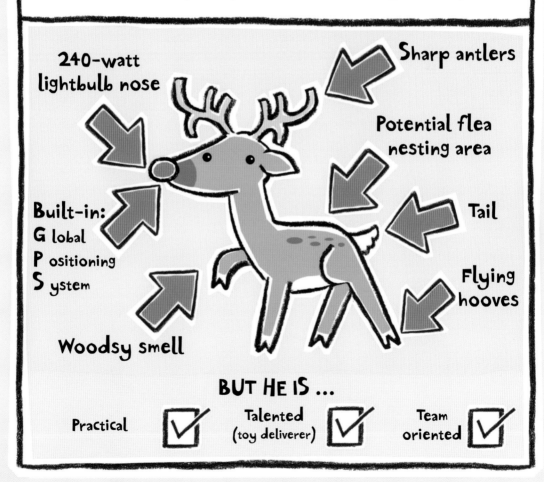

240-watt lightbulb nose

Sharp antlers

Potential flea nesting area

Built-in:
G lobal
P ositioning
S ystem

Tail

Flying hooves

Woodsy smell

BUT HE IS ...

Practical ✓

Talented (toy deliverer) ✓

Team oriented ✓

SANTA'S TEAM AND FLIGHT PLAN INCLUDES:

9 reindeer

| HELLO MY NAME IS: Rudolph | HELLO MY NAME IS: Dasher | HELLO MY NAME IS: Dancer | HELLO MY NAME IS: Prancer | HELLO MY NAME IS: Vixen | HELLO MY NAME IS: Comet | HELLO MY NAME IS: Cupid | HELLO MY NAME IS: Donner | HELLO MY NAME IS: Blitzen |

9 name tags

1 high-performance turbo sled

THIS SIDE UP

1 pretty humongous bag filled with toys

SANTA'S ROUTE:

Counterclockwise and at lightning speed!

ANTICIPATING A VISIT FROM SANTA, ARE YOU?

For optimal results, I suggest you leave an offering consisting of milk and cookies next to a window, door or unlit, I repeat, unlit fireplace.

A SCAREDY TIP!
Making Santa feel welcome can go a long way!

A FEW WAYS TO MAKE SANTA FEEL WELCOME AND AT HOME:

- Put out a welcome mat
- Play Christmas music for ambience
- Turn on air-conditioning
- Display poinsettia flower pots here and there
- Keep any pet with teeth at a safe distance

CHAPTER 6

CHRISTMAS
PET PEEVES

MISTLETOE

(SCAREDY'S TOP 10 WORST KISSING SCENARIOS)

1. Mistletoe above a piranha-infested pond.

2. Mistletoe above an anthill.

3. Mistletoe above a cactus.

4. Mistletoe above someone who hasn't just brushed their teeth!

5. Mistletoe above a drooling Chihuahua.

6. Mistletoe above a frozen metal post.

7. Mistletoe above a shark tank.

8. Mistletoe above a germ.

9. Mistletoe above a carnivorous plant.

10. Mistletoe above a high-voltage robot.

Nobody enjoys the risks involved when opening a present without knowing what it contains! These fail-proof, risk-free techniques to detect potential danger lurking in a box are my gift to you!

Five easy techniques to detect what is lurking inside a mysterious gift box:

1) **Stare at it.**
(Oddly shaped boxes are a clue you're in for a surprise.)

2) **Shake it.**
(Beware of spring mechanisms or loose parts.)

3) **Smell it.**
(A fishy smell means something smells fishy.)

4) **Listen to it.**
(Beeping or ticking should alert you. Really.)

5) **Send it.**
(To a lab for testing; get a second opinion.)

IMPORTANT NOTICE: These techniques do not instruct you to taste anything. Just needed to be clear on that!

A few scary gifts you may now avoid because you're a pro at detecting trouble:

lump of coal

jack-in-the-box

lunatic toy robot

blender

A SCAREDY TIP!

Airport security is always a good place to x-ray your gifts on the fly!

TINSEL GARLANDS
(TOP REASONS TO STOP THE MADNESS)

1. Too much sparkle can be blinding.

2. They can spiral out of control.

3. They will attract a disco crowd.

4. You can get tangled up.

5. Robots adore them.

HOLIDAY BITERS
(THE TOOTHY DUO TO AVOID)

The Nutcracker	Frostbite

At first glance, the nutcracker appears to be a practical device for nut lovers everywhere. But beware — underneath the shiny painted exterior lies an unreliable mechanism with a lot of bite!

Frostbite will nip you on the nose when you least expect it! Its tactic, passed down from generation to generation, relies entirely on surprising its victim. So, you must always be heavily clothed when you face its cold shoulder!

CHAPTER 7

CHRISTMAS
FUN

DRESSING UP

It's important to dress up for your holiday party. When you see loved ones you haven't seen in a while, you have to look your best and make a perfect lasting impression!

OPTION A:
The classic Christmas-themed sweater look

A popular choice for those who want to blend in with the Christmas scenery. A once-a-year deal (for some).

A SCAREDY TIP!
Purchase the Christmas-themed sweater on Boxing Day for an unbeatable bargain!

FYI, Boxing Day can be found in Canada, among other places

OPTION B:
The smart, preppy look

A basic combination of tie and sweater that inspires confidence, order and intellectual conversation.

OPTION C:
The cool, glitzy look

A bold statement with a lot of bling. There will be no question as to who's the star at the party!

OPTION D:
The Old Hollywood look

An extravagant choice for those who want to look sophisticated in a gown or tuxedo.

HOLIDAY ENTERTAINING

Entertaining is an art and not for the faint of heart.
Start figuring out whom you want to invite to your
Christmas party as early as July.

A SCAREDY TIP!

When making a guest list, try
to avoid inviting
individuals like piranhas
or double dippers.

- Prepare conversation starters on cue cards

- Avoid awkward topics

- Be on your best behavior

- Use coasters

- Cover the furniture in plastic

Avoid playing upbeat Christmas music;
it could lead to tap dancing.
Opt for ocean sounds to create a
calm, motionless atmosphere.

THE PARTY TIME CHART

(Fun-filled ideas to keep guests busy at the Christmas party)

Combine all of these options and your party will go smoothly!
If you're lucky, your guests will be napping in their seats
in no time, and cleanup will be a breeze!

CHAPTER 8

IF ALL
ELSE FAILS . . .

PLAY DEAD!

An uninvited Abominable Snowman was **NOT** part of the **PLAN**!

Playing Dead:
An anti-predator safety measure perfected by Scaredy Squirrel described as the act of remaining still or mimicking non-vital signs. This tactic ensures survival and allows danger to relocate. The Playing Dead exercise can take up to **2** hours.